Emerging from the Rubble

The Experiences of a Community on the Path to Heaven

By

David W. T. Bell and Dave Griffiths

Grosvenor House
Publishing Limited

All rights reserved
Copyright © David W.T. Bell and Dave Griffiths, 2021

The right of David W.T. Bell and Dave Griffiths to be
identified as the author of this
work has been asserted in accordance with Section 78
of the Copyright, Designs and Patents Act 1988

The book cover is copyright to David W.T. Bell and Dave Griffiths

This book is published by
Grosvenor House Publishing Ltd
Link House
140 The Broadway, Tolworth, Surrey, KT6 7HT.
www.grosvenorhousepublishing.co.uk

This book is sold subject to the conditions that it shall not, by way of
trade or otherwise, be lent, resold, hired out or otherwise circulated
without the author's or publisher's prior consent in any form of binding or
cover other than that in which it is published and
without a similar condition including this condition being imposed
on the subsequent purchaser.

A CIP record for this book
is available from the British Library

ISBN 978-1-83975-543-9

Dedication

To our families,

Thank you for your help,
understanding and support.

David Bell and Dave Griffiths

Acknowledgements

This work has been a joint collaboration. Dave Griffiths produced most of the storyline, and then we both revised the theology sections until they reflected our current beliefs. We have both gained enormously from the experience of writing this book. Our discussions frequently resulted in one or both of us developing fresh concepts, many of which have been incorporated in this work.

We are indebted to Susan Osman for her very helpful and detailed comments.

We are also very grateful to the many friends who gave us constructive hints and suggestions.

The cover has been produced by Joshua Palmer, we are fortunate to know such a talented illustrator.

Preface

I was introduced to Dave Griffiths when he mentioned his Facebook group 'Progressing Church' in another group. At the time I was investigating the concept that God is agape love and that all will be well in the end. Discussion within that group, and many others, has convinced me that everyone will be resurrected and eventually enjoy a good relationship with Jesus and their neighbours.

I suggested to Dave that a book exploring how this might be accomplished should be produced. He agreed to initially help me produce a book but over time it has become a joint collaboration.

The following story describes our vision of how a small part of God's plan might unfold. Our objective has been to present an interesting story that includes concepts that challenge conventional teachings. We think that the story gives an insight into a possible future, whilst completely accepting that many alternative views can be justified.

Some readers may find the concepts worthy of further investigation or discussion. We welcome

Love Above All Things

such discussions in the social media groups we have set up. These are listed at the end of the book.

We have enjoyed writing this story and hope that it brings reassurance and peace to all who read it.

David Bell
15 February 2021

1

Thomas studied his hands. He looked along both his forearms and swivelled his wrists. His hands felt and looked normal. This both surprised and comforted Thomas. Standing at six-foot one inch, Thomas was a slim man with black wavy hair. He reached up to his face and felt the roughness of a short beard.

Marvelling at how his newly resurrected body resembled his thirty-year-old self, he was pleased to find that he felt like himself, even though he was now alive again, many thousands of years after his 'first life'. He had been so caught up in the celebrations at the feast that he had not had a chance to really notice his new body until now.

"Wow, that was amazing," said Anne with a wistful smile.

Thomas looked to his left and grinned at Anne. She stood shoulder-high to him and looked wonderfully familiar to Thomas.

Anne was petite and had the warmest, most amazing dark brown eyes. She had a slightly shy nature; demure even. Anne and Thomas had first met in Anne's home. Even though this had happened many centuries ago, to Thomas and Anne it felt like just a few years ago.

"Totally awesome," replied Harmony.

Harmony was an American woman, with curly strawberry blonde hair and was an extrovert, with a motherly personality. She loved people easily and generously, and wherever she went she enthused others with her zest and enjoyment of life. Her laugh was loud and infectious, and she always seemed to find the funny side of everything. Her frame was thickset and curvy, which complimented her larger-than-life character.

"The most wonderful experience ever," said Yan.

Yan was a short Chinese man with thick straight dark brown hair. He had scars on his arms and back from where he had been tortured for leading an underground church in China. Yan had a cheerful personality that made it easy for him to make friends. He had a demeanour which was serene, and he was incredibly wise. He preferred to listen than to talk, and his travelling companions relished his insight.

Emerging from the Rubble

"It was so good to see him again," said Thomas.

Having just left the marriage supper, this small group found themselves sheltering beside the remains of a concrete apartment building. The sun was setting which made the stone buildings dotted around them radiate with a golden hue.

Harmony reflected on their recent experience. "The food was just exquisite and the wine, well Jesus certainly knows his wine."

"And there wasn't a top table. I saw Jesus serving food to some of his guests," said Yan with delight.

"Everyone was always thinking about how they could help the person next to them, handing them food or listening with genuine interest to what they were saying."

"I've never been in a room so full of love," said Anne.

"When Jesus asked who was ready to help him show love to the survivors still on earth, everyone stood and asked what they could do," said Yan.

*

The four had been given a specific destination by Jesus. It was a small community that was scratching an existence in a devastated city. The journey there was a chance for the new friends to bond with each other. They stood enjoying the warm sunshine that would soon make way to the dim light of the moon, heralding a cold night ahead.

"Let's gather some wood to make a fire," suggested Yan.

They all selected a different route into the surrounding area. There was rubble everywhere. So many buildings had been destroyed by the earthquakes, and the fighting. Collecting what they needed was not easy, and they were not helped by the fading light, but they each managed to find armfuls of wood and paper.

Yan had found some matches. He soon enticed welcome flames to dance over a tangle of wood. Sitting cross-legged around the growing warmth of the fire, they settled down and talked.

Harmony was excited to hear everyone's story. "My name is Harmony. I know Yan from conversations we had over Zoom many years ago, but I don't believe I have met the two of you before."

"My name is Anne. I was privileged to have Thomas stay in our house for a few nights and tell us of his experiences walking with Jesus," said Anne.

Emerging from the Rubble

"You must be the Apostle Thomas!" exclaimed Harmony. "I am so honoured to be in your presence."

"Please don't consider me to be anyone special," said Thomas. "I was helping the fishermen in our village when Jesus asked me to follow him. The experiences with him were incredible, but you already know so much about those three years with him from the gospel accounts. I would like to hear your stories."

Being resurrected was just like waking from sleep. Whatever had happened to their bodies had happened before they regained consciousness. It was like finding oneself in a perfectly healthy thirty-year-old body without any aches or pains.

The conversation between them flowed without the hinderance of ego. These men and women had been moulded by their life experiences to have empathy and compassion for other people. They were united by their love for Jesus, and the immeasurable honour of being among the first humans to be resurrected.

Thomas naturally seemed to provide gentle direction. He had been close to Jesus during his life and ministry. He had seen the things that the others had only heard and read about. The others were happy to defer to him. This made him uncomfortable as he had never considered himself a leader. He deeply trusted Anne, who had led a fledgling community in the decades after Jesus ascended.

"Go on Anne, share your story," Thomas gently coaxed Anne.

"I lived in a small village just north of Lake Galilee. I had a happy childhood. My father worked with horses and my mother knew how to make things from wool. When I became a woman, I married Benjamin, a kind man from a nearby family. Shortly after we were married, we heard the good news that God had come to earth as Jesus of Nazareth, the promised Messiah. When Thomas and his friend Bartholomew came to us on their journey, they told us all about their years with Jesus."

Thomas pursed his lips as he anticipated the next part of her story. He remembered the news reaching him all those years ago.

"We saw many come to believe in Jesus, and we met regularly at our house to discuss the good news, but the local leaders of the synagogue hated us meeting together. They arrested Benjamin and found him guilty of blasphemy."

Emerging from the Rubble

Anne fought back tears as she recalled those painful memories.

"They had him stoned to death. I was so distraught that for a few days I could not eat. I was encouraged and comforted by all who visited and supported me. We continued to meet, so they came for me."

Thomas, Yan, and Harmony were gripped by Anne's testimony. Only the crackle of the fire could be heard between her sentences.

"One day three men came into my house in the middle of the night. They dragged me out of bed and into my vegetable patch. The first rock hit my shoulder, the second hit the side of my head and stunned me. I don't remember the third. I must've died quickly. The next thing I knew, I was standing with all of you, in a crowd that included Jesus!"

"You were very courageous," said Thomas, wrapping his arm around her shoulder.

Yan and Harmony nodded with understanding.

"What about you, Harmony?" asked Anne.

Harmony glanced sideways and gathered her thoughts.

"You were very brave," she said. "Well, I grew up in a strict religious house. You know, no TV, no

Love Above All Things

radio except religious radio. I wasn't allowed to go to the cinema or the mall. I was told all sorts of things about God as a kid that scared the crap out of me. My folks wanted me to be a housewife, but I had other ideas.

I worked hard at school and got a place to study medicine. As soon as I moved out of the family home, I went a little crazy! At university I embraced my new freedom like a bat out of hell! Drinking, drugs, sleeping around. I just wanted to do all the things that I thought God would hate me for, because I hated God, you know?

But I could not shake Jesus offa me. He just seemed to keep turning up. I made some good friends who were believers but weren't religious. They liked to drink and talk about Jesus until the small hours. They liked to party, but it never got out of hand. They invited me to join a Facebook group and my eyes were opened to loads of ideas about God that I had never heard of before. It really changed everything for me. Soon I was talking to Jesus more than I ever had, and not because it was my duty, but because I loved to!"

"How did your family react?" asked Thomas.

"Well, at first they were horrified with my rejection of their religion. But, when I got my degree in

Emerging from the Rubble

medicine with first class honours, they started to see that I was ok. I went from there to volunteering in Yemen, helping get medicine to the victims of war over there. One day the hospital was shelled and the last thing I remember was the window blowing in and everything going black. Then, like you Anne, I'm waking up in my body with you all, just before the marriage meal!"

"Wow," said Anne, "you died serving others. You really gave your life for love!"

"I guess so," replied Harmony, "but it didn't feel like that at the time. You just… get on with what you know is right, you know?"

Harmony turned to Yan, who sat next to her, listening to everyone, and occasionally adding more wood to the fire. "And Yan, how about you?"

Yan took a deep breath. "My story is a bit long," he laughed self-consciously. "I am so used to hiding my true feelings I am not sure where to start."

"Go on," coaxed Anne, making sure she made eye contact to reassure Yan.

"Well, I will start at the end." Yan threw a large log on to the fire. The flames lit up the concrete walls, making their shadows dance.

Love Above All Things

"They shot me with three others. They came in one morning before the sun came up and took us. They read out the charges of sedition against the government to a small crowd of locals they had rounded up. We were shot in front of them at the sports stadium."

"Who were 'they'?" asked Thomas.

"The secret police, and those loyal to the government in my country. The rulers hated our communities because they knew we believed in a power higher than theirs. We met together as often as we could to learn about the kingdom of God and encourage each other to always show love to our neighbours."

"The powers in our time were the same," said Anne. "People usually hate what they can't control." All four of them nodded silently.

"I come from a poor family. My brothers and I had to work in the factory to support our parents. My father died when I was twelve and my mother found a new husband who was much older. He was violent. My two brothers drank too much, and I felt very alone.

When I was eighteen, I heard about God's love from a man my age I knew from my village. He

Emerging from the Rubble

invited me to a secret meeting, and I felt the love of God in my body. I experienced the power of God and I was never the same again. Suddenly I felt free and could see a better way to live, much better than just obeying the orders of the government. I kept working in the factory but wanted to spend more and more time with the community. They became my family. The older members were so kind and wise, and the younger ones were just like me. We did all we could to tell people how God loves us, and that Jesus' way leads to inner peace. The community grew quickly."

Harmony nodded her head in agreement. She had seen how people in war zones had been so comforted by the love of God, and how they had been able to face suffering with the hope of a peaceful future. Yan and Harmony had become friends in the age of the Internet. Their lives had been lived out in the late twentieth and early twenty-first centuries. Connecting with each other due to a passion for social justice, they had become confidants. Yan had been a great source of comfort to Harmony when she was rejected by her family, and Yan had also gained a lot of comfort by talking to Harmony when he was being persecuted for helping members of his community.

Love Above All Things

"The good news travelled to nearby towns and villages and I found myself spending many evenings passing on what I knew to other people. But, the secret police were watching the communities, and I was taken in for questioning many times. They began to torture me. At first it was making me stay awake for days on end. Then they began to beat me. The last time they took me in, they used electric shocks. I sometimes felt abandoned and lonely, but the love I had in my heart for the communities gave me strength. I never told the secret police what they wanted to hear."

Anne was visibly moved by Yan's story. It reminded her of her own life, being constantly worried that the authorities would arrest her.

"They let me go after a while, and things went quiet for some years. I was able to see the communities grow stronger and trust Jesus more deeply. It was a great joy, the way people came into the family of faith and were transformed by the love of the people around them. The sadness came when some people loyal to the government found our groups, and told the local officials about who was in them.

Then the dark day came. Many people were taken from their homes and put in a 're-education camp'.

Emerging from the Rubble

The leaders, including me, were proclaimed as traitors to our country and dangerous. That is when we were taken to the stadium and shot. The last thing I remember was the loud bang of the gun and then nothing. I didn't feel any pain."

Yan began to chuckle, his shoulders bouncing with joy.

"And then I found myself standing in a crowd of people and Jesus was there in the mist of us all. I looked across the crowd and I saw people I knew who had also died for leading the communities and sharing news about the kingdom of heaven. You were all there, too?"

Anne was wiping tears from her face. "Yes, Yan. We were there with you. We were called up to the great feast with Jesus, too. People from every country across history were called. People who overcame the temptation to depart from the way."

Yan turned to Thomas. "What happened with you?"

"After the Holy Spirit came to us in the upper room, we felt a new power. That's when we started to go our different ways. A few of us went north at first. The road was easy at first, and we rejoiced greatly in the things we had seen and experienced. We were happy just to make light

Love Above All Things

conversation with the people we talked to. We waited for the Spirit to show us what to say. We left Andrew in a small town near Nazareth, where he found it felt natural for him to share the good news. He had old friends nearby who were already believers, for they had also seen the amazing things Jesus had done. Bartholomew and I continued north, and soon after met Anne and Benjamin. They were so ready to hear more about the Kingdom of Heaven. So, we stayed with them for some time."

"It was the happiest time of our lives," blushed Anne. "We learned so much and began to know the power of the Spirit."

"After a few days Bartholomew decided to stay in the region to support the small communities that were being formed. I understood that I had to go further east. I was asked to take the good news outside the Roman world. I began a daily practice of waking early, and praying while walking, opening my heart to the Spirit. I got used to sensing peace, or resistance. It helped me determine where I should spend my day, and who to be with.

I managed to stay away from the authorities who were harassing the communities of faith. After

Emerging from the Rubble

some months I eventually reached India and stayed there, spreading news of the Kingdom of Heaven. It was received with joy by many people, and I made wonderful friends and saw many beautiful things.

However, there was opposition from some people in India, and one group hated me for being a foreigner challenging their traditions. They ambushed me on a hill where I went to pray and seek the Spirit. I was killed by a blow from a sword, but like you all I did not suffer in my death. I remember feeling shocked at the sensation of the blade inside my body, but excitement at the same time because I felt sure that God would receive my spirit. Also like you, the next thing I knew was that I am in my body again, but it is younger and stronger, and I was standing before Jesus."

"And now here we are," said Thomas. "Alive again, just as he promised we would be!"

"And we are joining him in bringing good news to the world again," laughed Yan.

"Being, good news," added Harmony. "We get to work with God in this time of great suffering and uncertainty. Whatever happened after we had all died, it must have been truly awful. The cities are in ruins, and the population is a tenth of what it was when Yan and I were alive."

"Yes, everyone has been forced to live in small communities, totally dependent on what they and their neighbours can produce," said Yan. "The infrastructure that used to provide water, electricity and the Internet has been destroyed."

"It does however present the opportunity to regenerate society with a more compassionate framework," said Harmony.

"Well, that's why we are here," said Anne. "To help everyone recognise God's love for all and accept his guidance in their lives. Bit by bit, we will see it happen, and I can't wait!"

2

Yan and Thomas were several yards ahead of Harmony and Anne when the first peal of thunder tore across the leaden sky above them. Within a few seconds they were soaked to the skin by lashing rain.

"Aaah, the supplies will get wet!" shouted Harmony, trying to make herself heard above the noise of the storm. Yan looked back and motioned towards a small building several rows of trees away. The friends did their best to leap over the irrigation channels and not slip on the wet clay soil. They were soon sheltered under the leaking roof of an old, abandoned hut.

"Why did Jesus put us so far from the community?" asked Harmony.

Thomas looked at her with a kind expression. "I agree this journey could have been shorter. However to be accepted, we must appear to be true travellers."

Harmony furthered her thoughts. "Sorry, I agree. Walking will help us understand the landscape. So

Love Above All Things

often we miss things in our haste to achieve our current task."

The other three nodded their agreement. The city lay another twenty miles away and none of them knew exactly what they would find there.

"Jesus said we must come as strangers. We must be reluctant to proclaim who we are or why we are here. We come to help them and to encourage them to love through showing kindness to us and others." Harmony was repeating the instructions they had received at the Marriage Supper of the Lamb.

"Yes," said Yan. "Jesus wants genuine empathy and love to grow in the hearts of those who remain. We cannot demand it of them. We cannot expect special treatment. We must seek to serve and not be served."

"Remember that these people have suffered terribly and the life they are now experiencing is completely different to the life they had only ten years ago," said Thomas. "The inevitable consequences of the impact that humans were having on the environment has destroyed all the economies, obliterated all governments and reduced everyone in the world to subsistence

Emerging from the Rubble

survival in small groups. They are now resigned to being completely reliant on their own efforts."

The rain eased and the four travellers continued their journey. With mud covered legs, bedraggled hair and sweating from the humidity, they began to pass derelict apartment blocks and shops long since raided and torched.

Thomas stopped and stared. Before him, a whole wall was missing from what was once a hospital. Scores of beds stretched down the long concourse of the building. It had been abandoned when the electricity failed and the medicines were exhausted.

Concrete boulders and broken glass lay everywhere. Abandoned cars now littered the road.

"What happened?" asked Thomas.

Yan had gone around to the side of the building. "Come and see!" he called.

The other three joined him and Yan pointed at a huge crack in the ground that ran from underneath the building away into the overgrown bush in the middle distance.

"Many earthquakes," said Yan quietly. "They brought down all the buildings."

Love Above All Things

The journey continued and the cracks in the ground got worse, and the destruction around them increased. The mood was sombre as the four friends got used to seeing human remains in various horrific scenarios.

As they passed from the suburbs to the city, it was clear that the destruction had been almost total.

Yan took a long drink of water and looked around sadly as they began to assemble camp for their second night on the road.

Anne was overwhelmed by all she had seen. "I never imagined that people would live in such vast cities. All those people. All those lives. It must've been so terrible at the end," she said with a steady stream of tears running down her cheeks.

Harmony sat beside her. She stroked her hair and lifted her face toward her. "It must've been awful, but sweet Anne, it was not the end. It was the inevitable destiny of that age, but a new day is here for the Earth."

Thomas' heart swelled to see how much Harmony clearly loved Anne. "Every dead body we saw today will be raised," he added. "This isn't the end for them, and the Lord will restore all that was lost."

Emerging from the Rubble

Anne wiped away her tears, "It's true! I believe it!"

"I saw a lot of death," reflected Yan. "It never gets easier, but it does remind us that our Father's desire is to bring everyone back to life."

"Life in abundance," said Harmony, squeezing Anne until she managed a smile.

They slept in the glow of a fire, refreshed by the conversation.

*

The morning came with the breaking of the best bread they had ever tasted. It had been included in the provisions that Jesus had given them for the journey.

"How long do you think we will be here?" Thomas asked Yan as they warily scanned the darkened windows of the empty buildings.

"As long as it takes," Yan said slowly. "Jesus said we can go back to Jerusalem to get rest and encouragement when we need to. He said that all our effort must flow from trusting that he will ensure that all will be well. He encouraged us to always have patience."

"That's good," chuckled Thomas, "He was never in a hurry when I was walking around Israel with him."

Love Above All Things

A few streets further into the city there began to be signs of life. A faint plume of smoke was drifting up into the low-lying grey cloud, and the echo of dogs barking somewhere nearby added to the eerie atmosphere.

"Stop! No further!" A shadowy figure in a third story window called down.

"We come in peace," shouted Harmony, raising her hands and the others did the same.

"Stay there!" commanded the voice. "We have guns, and we will not hesitate to use them!"

Five men in dusty grey clothes filed out from the building and surrounded the four friends.

"Who are you?" asked one of them as he patted Thomas down, looking for weapons.

"We have come from the east. We are looking for shelter. We are prepared to join any community that will have us," responded Thomas, as he tried to make eye contact with the man.

"My name is Thomas. This is Yan, Harmony and Anne. We have only recently found each other, and we are looking for some sanctuary. Can you help us?"

Emerging from the Rubble

The man looked back up towards the window where the first voice had come from.

"Bring them in," called the voice.

The courtyard was full of activity. As the men led the friends through the arch they could see children adding wood to the fires, and women silently stirring cooking pots and washing clothes. Older men sat in a circle, passing a solitary cigarette from one to another, taking it in turns to inhale the stale smelling smoke. Weary eyes cautiously scrutinised the friends. Not a word was said, nor a smile exchanged.

Inside the largest building a dimly lit lobby area formed a sort of office in which were a desk, a few safes against the wall, and a row of lockers. A man stood behind the desk with his hands touching the wooden desktop. He looked tired and had scars on his face.

"Why do you have no weapons?" he asked tersely.

"We have come in peace. We want no trouble," answered Anne.

The man looked cynically at his companions.

"No trouble?" he laughed sarcastically. "We've had nothing but trouble for fuck knows how long!"

Love Above All Things

"We know. Don't we all want a better future?" Anne summoned her courage to look the man in the eye, as she responded as gently and sincerely as she could.

"So, you want sanctuary? Why did you choose us?" the man demanded.

"You were the city on our road forward," replied Yan truthfully, but tactfully choosing not to be more specific.

"I see," said the man, looking intently at his desk. "You may stay here for a few nights," he said briskly. "They call me Owl. These men will find you a room to share. What provisions do you have?"

Owl pointed at the bags that Thomas and Yan were carrying. Reluctantly, they surrendered the bags to Owl's men who immediately opened them. Some torches, some batteries, a few bags of seeds, extra clothing and some bread were laid out on the desk.

"Wait!" said Yan. "I also have this..." He bent down and peeled back his sock to reveal a gold tie pin. The others offered up their gold and silver items of jewellery, too.

Emerging from the Rubble

"Jewellery?" exclaimed Owl with genuine surprise. "These are so precious! Why would you give these to me? We didn't know you had them, and you could've kept them for yourselves?"

"We come in peace. We want to trust you, and for you to trust us." Yan handed Owl the items.

Owl looked at Yan and for the first time, his mouth cracked a wry smile. "Interesting," he said.

Owl's men ushered the friends away from the lobby area and escorted them up several flights of stairs and along dingy corridors until they arrived at a room.

Silently the door was pushed open and the friends were ushered in without a word. There were three bunk beds without mattresses, but with blankets wrapped around the frames.

"This will do," said Harmony determined to remain positive about the circumstances. She turned to Anne and grabbed her hand. "Come on, let's beat the boys to the top bunks!" she laughed, and they threw themselves on to the beds.

Thomas looked at Yan with a grin. "Let's get some rest" he said.

*

Love Above All Things

At 6am there was a heavy banging on the door. Owl strode in without warning and loudly cleared his throat.

"You must get up and be ready in the next thirty minutes. You two men will join the scavenging team looking for supplies in the next city. Women, you will be going to the river to fetch water. Food is available at six thirty in the courtyard. If you're not in line, you do not eat."

The friends got up and dressed without any fuss and headed down to the courtyard. A drab mass of people were sat round sipping steaming hot water and eating flatbread. After receiving their portion, Yan and Thomas were directed toward a group of younger looking men, who were sat together.

"May we sit here?" whispered Yan to a wiry young man who looked to be about twenty years old. The man looked up from his flatbread in surprise.

"Yes, you can," he said quietly. He watched as Yan and Thomas took their places by his side. "I am Yan, and this is Thomas," said Yan after a slightly awkward pause.

"Hello," said the young man. "They call me Polecat. I think it's because I am tall and skinny

Emerging from the Rubble

and can get into places others can't," he said, with a hint of a smile.

"So, we have met Owl, and now Polecat," replied Thomas. "Why do you call each other by the names of creatures?" he asked.

"Owl started it. I think it's because our old names remind us all of times that we will never see again. Times before all of the suffering, when we had families and jobs and food and..." Polecat trailed off as he began to remember life before everything had broken down. "It's easier just to be someone else now," he said, pulling himself together.

"Is Owl in charge then?" enquired Yan.

"Yes. He used to be Chief of Police here in the city. He never married or had children, and he stayed in the city as things got worse and worse. The people follow him because he showed such loyalty to the city."

"That makes sense. Do you like him?" Yan continued.

"I respect him, but he is very harsh. I am afraid of him. I've seen him kill people who didn't obey his rules. He controls all of the weapons and his men are very loyal to him. Most of them are his former police officers who either lost their families or brought them here under his protection. Don't mess with him. That's my advice!" Polecat looked as if he had said too much, and quickly finished his flatbread.

"Are you coming to the town?" he asked.

"Yes, we have been told to," said Thomas, finishing his flatbread. "What should we expect?"

"A long day of nothing much," said Polecat with resignation in his voice. "If we are lucky we will find an apartment with some food left in the cupboards, or some cigarettes in the basement of an old shop."

Yan and Thomas followed Polecat out to meet the other men, who numbered about forty in total.

After the men had left the encampment, a subdued hush fell over the courtyard. The women who were left continued their tasks, barely speaking to each other.

Anne and Harmony had instinctively headed toward a makeshift play area, where some younger women, who appeared to be mothers, or at least guardians, watched over five small children as they played make believe with some very battered toys.

Emerging from the Rubble

"How old?" asked Anne, motioning at a young boy who was building a tower of pebbles.

The young woman answered meekly, "He is only just six, and the youngest child here."

Anne nodded with understanding and smiled at the little boy who quickly returned a toothy grin.

"My name is Sylvia," she offered, touching her heart. "This is Alex. His father died years ago," she continued in a surprising outpouring of her personal story.

"I'm so sorry," Harmony responded.

"We have all lost so much. Not one child here has a family like we did when we were their age," said Sylvia in an emotionless voice.

"It's all we can do to give them a chance to play, once in the morning and once just before evening meal."

"Are you from this city?" asked Anne.

"Yes," answered Sylvia, "we all are. Owl doesn't welcome outsiders. In fact, I'm shocked he's allowed you to stay! No one from outside has ever been allowed in."

Love Above All Things

Harmony looked at Anne. "We are so grateful for the shelter, and we offered him our precious items straight away," she said to Sylvia.

"Yes, well, that will keep him happy for a short time," sighed Sylvia. "Take my advice. If he wants you to give yourself to him or any of his men, just go along with it. Resistance could cost you your life."

Sylvia suddenly seemed to withdraw into herself and stared at the ground.

"He's hurt you?" asked Harmony, gently.

"Either he or his men have hurt all of us," said Sylvia, her voice a monotone, while still staring wide-eyed at the ground.

"We women are playthings for them. Apart from the wives of his police officers we have all lost our husbands and boyfriends. If they weren't already dead, Owl saw to it that none of us had any family left to defend us."

Sylvia suddenly panicked. "I've said too much!" she gasped.

Anne reached over and put her hand on Sylvia's forearm. "Thank you for the warning," she said quietly but firmly. "We won't forget this."

3

"You two new boys, listen up!" shouted Owl as the men stood around talking quietly. Everyone fell silent when Owl began to speak.

"You don't know how this works, and you only have one chance to learn. We move quickly, in groups of four. Each group takes a street and works from house to house. Be as quiet as possible. You are looking for food items, weapons or tools. If you find anyone alive, bring them to me for assessment. If you find anyone sick, kill them. If you meet resistance, kill them. Move on quickly. Don't think about it, just act and move on."

Yan and Thomas looked at each other with a deep knowing in their eyes. They knew that this would be a challenging day. Suddenly one of Owl's men had his arm to their backs and was ushering them toward Owl.

"You two are with me," said Owl. "You Polecat! With us!" he shouted at Polecat who quickly came over. "Polecat knows the ropes," said Owl.

A half hour's brisk march away lay a satellite town of the main city.

Love Above All Things

"You must've been through this town before?" Thomas quietly asked Polecat as they walked.

Polecat sighed, "Too many times," he said wearily. "Owl insists we keep coming back, over and over. Sometimes I think it's just to give us something to do, to give us something like structure. Sometimes we do find something new, but mostly we don't."

"So, Owl makes you do things purely for the sake of discipline?" asked Yan.

"That's right. He says it is good for our minds and bodies. I just wish we could move further out. Hey, did you pass anywhere exciting when you came to us? You must've seen things?" Polecat suddenly seemed genuinely interested.

"We have seen many things," said Yan, "but not really anything we can report for plundering."

"Didn't you have to take things for your own survival?" Polecat replied.

"We believe that if we show kindness, and trust in people, we are looked after," Thomas answered.

"You have so much trust! How can you be so sure you won't be overcome by those more powerful? The world is cruel!"

Emerging from the Rubble

"Yes, it is. But Yan, Anne, Harmony, and I met because we believe in love and life. We want to put others first as best as we can, and to see the good in people." Thomas tried to smile a warm smile to demonstrate sincerity to Polecat, but Polecat was perplexed and seemed slightly amused by the whole idea.

At the edge of the town Owl halted the men and motioned the teams of four to fan out and go to their designated streets. He called forward Polecat, Thomas, and Yan.

"Come," he said sternly. "Let's go. I have something to show you."

They walked in silence for several minutes until they came to a depot that was full of deteriorating buses. Owl led them to one bus and said, "Watch this," with a glint of pride in his eyes.

He slammed his hand on the bus door, violently pushing it open. Inside could be heard the scurrying of people and worried, whispered voices. Owl climbed into the bus and clapped his hands.

"Today is the day!" he shouted. "You have resisted too long."

Love Above All Things

His announcement was met with cries of distress from men and women further down the vehicle.

Owl disappeared into the bus and then re-emerged at the door gripping a young woman. She was dirty and her clothes were almost in rags.

Owl yanked her down the step. "Go in and get the others," he ordered. "They are coming back with us."

Polecat immediately went up into the bus in obedience, but turned back when he realised he was not being followed by Thomas and Yan.

"Go on!" yelled Owl. "This wretched family have been refusing to leave this hole and join us for years, and now they must be taken by force."

"Why can they not stay here if they want to?" asked Thomas.

"Are you really questioning me?" Owl retorted with disdain. "Go up there and get them, now!"

Polecat scurried to the back of the bus and a scuffle could be heard. He then came out of the bus with a very thin man who he gripped by the hair, and with his arm wrenched behind his back, as if he was under arrest.

Emerging from the Rubble

"There are two more. Now get in there!" scowled Owl through gritted, angry teeth.

"We don't use force," said Yan calmly.

Owl's temper snapped. He released his grip on the young woman who fell to the ground, and he pushed his chest aggressively against Yan's.

"You don't use force?" he sneered. Before Yan knew what was happening, he found himself on the ground, Owl standing over him.

"Perhaps you need to know that I am in charge here," Owl barked.

In a rapid, forceful movement, Owl brought his foot down hard onto Yan's stomach, knocking the breath out of him. Yan groaned with a mixture of pain, and desperation for air. Owl stepped over him and smashed his boot into Yan's ribs. Yan rolled over, fighting for breath. Owl lashed out and kicked Yan in the face. Yan's nose burst and blood ran into his mouth. He fell backwards with the force of the kick and lay on the floor, the fearful crying of the bus woman becoming a strange echo as his consciousness wavered.

After only a few moments, the pain in Yan's body receded and he regained consciousness. His wounds stopped bleeding and he stood to his feet calmly and unaided.

Owl was confused. The two friends stood before him, with no threat of reprisal. Distracted by the sudden violence, Polecat in panic had let go of his captive, who had quickly fled the depot with the other three bus dwellers.

Owl quickly realised his plan had failed, and he had been made to look weak. His fury was now directed at Polecat.

"You let them go, you fool!" he screamed, drawing out a police baton from his belt. He threatened to smash it into Polecat's head. Yan quickly moved in front of Polecat. Wiping the residual blood from his top lip, Yan passively challenged Owl and protected Polecat.

Owl was humiliated. He raised the baton again but hesitated, his feet shuffling slightly in the dirt.

"It's ok," said Yan softly, still looking at Owl with his compassionate eyes.

By now, Thomas had joined Yan and was standing by his side, shielding Polecat.

Owl exhaled loudly, his frustration obvious. He sheathed the baton, straightened his shirt, and

Emerging from the Rubble

stepped forward, closing in on Thomas and Yan. With his sweating face just millimetres from theirs, he clenched his teeth again.

"Don't forget who runs this place. I have killed insubordinates before, and I wouldn't think twice about dispatching you, and your female friends."

Owl spat on the ground and turned away, walking out of the depot into the heat of the day.

Polecat was trying to understand what had just happened.

"I would say thank you, but I am so scared of Owl!" he stammered. He took a huge lungful of air, then immediately softened. "But, thank you. No-one has ever protected me in my whole life. Why did you do that for me? Who am I to you?"

"You'd do the same for us," said Thomas, with a strange certainty in his voice.

Polecat felt a tear slide down his cheek, for the first time since he was a child. Somewhere deep in his heart, he believed that he would. Was this what it felt like to be loved?

4

"The men will be back soon," said Sylvia, looking at the sky. The light was just beginning to fade. Some of the other women were finishing the preparation of food on the other side of the courtyard.

"When they come back, they are always so exhausted. They eat and then they usually want some sort of distraction. That's when we take turns up there…"

Sylvia glanced upwards towards the top floor of the block.

"Owl will put you on the rota soon," she said, without emotion. Sylvia seemed determined to be matter of fact about the fact that the women were being forced into sexual slavery.

Harmony got up and signalled to Anne that she wanted to talk. They found the quietest part of the courtyard.

"How do we deal with this?" sighed Harmony, not directly asking Anne.

Emerging from the Rubble

Anne shook her head at the horror of what could happen.

"Jesus told us that God had had to give everyone the desire to procreate and the desire to protect themselves and their community," Anne explained.

"Yeah, I mean, that's how we make babies," mused Harmony.

"I wonder what role sex will play in the future?" Anne pondered. "I feel we are here to suppress these violent desires and encourage everyone to realise that they can live a different way."

"Sex can be so beautiful," answered Harmony, "But only when there is consent, respect, commitment - not like this. Not when it's forced. That's rape."

The two women sat in prayerful thought for several minutes.

*

After the evening meal, a tense atmosphere descended on the camp. Anne and Harmony were now reunited with Yan and Thomas.

"Do you remember when we first met?" Thomas asked Anne. "Do you remember how we explained the cost of being a disciple, and what it means to live in Agape love?"

Anne nodded with a soft smile.

"All that Jesus showed us, all he taught, it's as true now as it ever was, but now it is more possible to live that way," Thomas continued.

"What happened to your face, Yan?" asked Harmony. "You have dried blood all over your shirt and in your nose?"

"We refused to take people from the next town," said Yan. "Owl could not control his anger and beat me, but the pain stopped almost immediately. My body does not hurt or ache, though there are signs of wounding."

Yan was impressed with his resurrected body's ability to heal so quickly.

"They may beat us, and we know we may suffer temporarily, but we are here in the humble power of Agape love. We can be sure hearts will change in time."

The conversation was broken by Anne suddenly becoming aware that two women were being escorted up the stairs.

"What is it?" asked Yan.

Emerging from the Rubble

"Those women are on the rota tonight. They are to give their bodies to some of the men. I'm told it happens most days. Harmony, we must do something."

"Do you want us to come too?" asked Thomas.

"No, we will call you if we need you," said Anne. They tentatively followed the other women up the stairs.

As Harmony and Anne reached the top floor corridor, they realised that only one door was shut. Approaching the door, they could hear the sound of two men talking.

Harmony reached out and knocked on the door. The voices inside became quiet. Harmony knocked once more and waited. Suddenly the door was opened and there stood an older man with his belt undone. Behind him stood another man who looked confused at the interruption.

"Yes?" said the man bluntly.

Harmony smiled and asked, "Can we come in?"

"Why, is it buy one get one free tonight?" laughed the man.

Love Above All Things

"Buying something means it is worth something, right?" said Harmony. "Yet you don't pay for this. These ladies are here out of pure duress."

The man pulled his belt out from his trousers and folded it in half in his hands, to form a weapon.

Before he could speak or do anything, Harmony continued.

"Did you ever know your mother? Did you have a sister? A wife? A daughter?"

The man became still and lowered the belt.

"I see kindness in you," said Harmony delicately.

Suddenly the man behind him strode forward and pushed Harmony out of the door.

"What? You want to stay and watch?" he growled at Anne.

Anne looked over at the women, who were both extremely anxious and agitated. One of them shook her head rapidly, as if to plead with Anne to leave them alone.

"We've all lost loved ones," Anne said looking at both men in turn. "I am no different. My husband is dead. I know we get lonely. Is my friend right? Is there kindness in you?"

Emerging from the Rubble

The first man lunged at Anne with his belt, but Anne instinctively moved out of the way. It was only a matter of centimetres, but it was enough to avoid the assailant's intention.

Anne looked at the man.

"Kindness," she said simply. She turned, exited the room, and joined Harmony.

The door was slammed shut. As Anne and Harmony began heading toward the stairs, the door opened again, and the second man pushed past the friends.

"You bitches have ruined my night!" he spat at them.

Anne grabbed Harmony's hand and pulled her back toward the room.

On re-entering the room, they found the other man sat on a bed frame, tears rolling down his face. The belt lay on the floor and the two women were in the far corner, huddled together and unsure what to do.

Harmony looked at them, "It's ok. You can go."

The women gingerly walked past the crying man and went on their way.

Love Above All Things

Harmony turned to the man and he looked up at her.

"My wife. My beautiful daughters," he sobbed.

The following two hours was spent by his side as the two friends listened to his story of loss and pain.

"They call him Rabbit," reported Anne to Thomas and Yan as the friends met up later that night in their room.

"Because he had so many children," added Harmony. "Some of them are dead, but some may be alive in a different part of the city. Their mother died early in the fighting that happened here after the great migration."

"People are so frequently judged without their full story being understood," reflected Thomas. "All he needed was to be reminded of his true humanity, and he could see what he was doing was wrong. We must remember this."

*

A few days later Sylvia approached Anne. "You seem to understand what has happened to the world. Can you explain why there has been so much devastation, so many deaths?"

Emerging from the Rubble

Anne thought for a while, "What or who do you think is responsible?" she asked.

Sylvia replied, "If I believed in God, I would blame him. They told us in Sunday School that he was an all-caring father who would always protect us. Life has been so shit since then that that lie has been resolutely nailed."

Anne gently replied, "I understand your feelings".

"You don't believe in God either then?" replied Sylvia, looking up at Anne.

"It depends on what you mean by 'God'. I believe in a father who doesn't dictate what we do. I don't believe in a puppet-master God. I would say God was not responsible. We were. Humankind had been abusing the planet for so long that all the mechanisms that were in place to keep the environment healthy and balanced for us were overwhelmed. Eventually the temperatures rose, the ice melted, some earthquakes and volcanoes were triggered, and you know the result."

"So your God couldn't stop all this?" said Sylvia indignantly.

"God could have stopped a lot of things, had he had enough friends listening to his voice. The global devastation has been enormous, but from

Love Above All Things

these ashes a better environment can now be created. Before all this happened the economies and governments of all the countries in the world were failing. They had all become corrupt, benefitting a few, at the expense of the many. A tiny number of people were becoming extremely wealthy while the vast majority were struggling, a good many in refugee camps. However hard people of good will tried to correct these imbalances, the forces of the powerful were always able to overcome their efforts.

"I believe that God is incredibly sad that so many have suffered, and that many are still suffering. But the new environment means that everyone is starting now with nothing. Everyone is more or less equal to everyone else. The chance to build a much better society for all is open to us, if we take this opportunity."

"I hope you are right," said Sylvia. "Currently all I can see is suffering and hardship ahead."

5

Just as the sun was beginning to lighten the sky, and a few sleepy birds were beginning to greet the day, Thomas was pulled from his bed. With a rough hand over his mouth, he was dragged out of the room and along the corridor.

"Owl wants to see you," said one of the men.

Thomas nodded calmly and the men cautiously loosened their grip on him and began escorting him down the stairs.

Owl stood looking out of the window, the sunrise breaking before him beyond the distant hills.

"These seeds," he said. "What are they?"

"There are all kinds," answered Thomas. "Grain, corn, fruit trees and vegetables. My old friend is a gardener. He entrusted the seeds to us."

"I see," said Owl. "And now I have them. Do you trust me with them?"

"Owl, we need to talk about yesterday."

Owl suddenly became uncomfortable.

Love Above All Things

"That's all I needed to know. If they are food seeds, we will plant them and farm them. You can go now."

With a flick of his fingers, his two men opened the door to the courtyard and Thomas found himself alone with a blue sky above him. He looked at the way the sunlight was playing on the clouds and his heart swelled.

"My Father," he whispered. And that was all he needed to say. As if waking from a dream, Thomas found himself standing on a balcony overlooking Jerusalem. Next to him stood Jesus.

"You're doing so well," said Jesus with a warm smile. He laid his hand on Thomas's shoulder. Thomas looked at the hand and could plainly see the pink scar on Jesus' wrist. For a brief moment Thomas remembered how he had doubted that Jesus was indeed back from the grave, and how he had reached out to touch the scars for himself.

"Lord, the people are so broken. There is so much loss, so much sadness. There is abuse and there is violence."

"They are still driven by their old desires. You must understand that it takes many years for some people to see the way of love. We are in this for

Emerging from the Rubble

the long haul." Jesus sounded both reassuring and resolute. "Papa and I know that, in time, everyone will come to see that unfailing love holds all things together. Love gives creation its meaning. You and the others have been perfected by love. You now embody it wherever you go and whoever you are with. Think of the individuals you are reaching. They understand a little more each day. Have faith, my friend. Every human life is an expression of our divine love. It's just that some have not discovered this yet."

"Will it be the same on the new earth?" asked Thomas.

"To begin with the new earth will be similar in many ways to your current environment. Once the new earth is formed, I will start resurrecting people that died on the old earth. I will assess each person, for example how well they gave drinks to the poor, visited people in prison and so on and decide which group they should be assigned to. No group will be larger than five hundred people, and many will be only one to two hundred in size. Helpers such as yourself will be assigned to each group and will have the same role you currently have, to encourage everyone in their community to operate from a position of love rather than selfishness.

Love Above All Things

"Some groups will have particularly difficult characters and it will take us a very long time to convince them that they are loved, and that it is safe for them to consider others as friends, not just an entity to be exploited.

"Other groups will be full of kind people. Many in these groups will quickly accept that Papa is a good father and that they can trust him. I will call some of the people in these groups to become helpers, and then they will be trained by being assigned to groups with established helpers. As the number of helpers grows, I will be able to resurrect more people and create further groups.

"Eventually everyone who has ever existed will be resurrected and live in a group on the new earth. After perhaps a long time everyone in every group will accept that Papa is their good and loving Father, and that he cares for them and will ensure that they are always safe and can be at peace."

"You describe a wonderful future. I wish it could happen more quickly! I wish I could stay with you!" cried Thomas, wrapping his arms around Jesus. Jesus held him tight and rubbed his back, comfortingly.

Emerging from the Rubble

"I know," he said. "You will see me again soon. For now, you have more hearts to illuminate with love. Be patient with Owl. He is just as loved as you are!"

Thomas nodded. Suddenly he was back in the courtyard, staring at the sky. A few men and women were beginning to prepare the food for breakfast.

Thomas smiled to himself while he looked around, basking in the glow of having been with Jesus.

*

Seeds were planted. Crops and trees began to grow. Slowly, and with regular signs that progress was being made, the culture in the community began to change. Since Harmony and Anne had intervened, fewer men were taking advantage of the rota. Some couples began to form, and this brought joy to everyone. Harmony and Anne loved to spend time with the womenfolk, joining in with their various tasks.

The coming months saw faces begin to lighten, and people becoming happier. The friends began to find the sense of humour within the people. They worked out who liked practical jokes, who laughed at puns, and who giggled at slapstick.

Love Above All Things

The friends delighted in this, and the sound of laughter began to echo across the courtyard and along the corridors of the block.

"Joy makes everything seem easier," remarked Sylvia one day. She and Anne were watching a group of men and women having a water fight whilst watering the crops. She knew that such light-hearted things would not have occurred if Thomas, Yan, Harmony and Anne had not joined the community.

"Yes, there is fun to be had in the work," said Anne.

As the harvests came in, the community became wise in how to live seasonally. People with no previous experience of working the land soon became well versed in the practices that gave them food. Rainwater was collected and either channelled to the crops or stored to be boiled before being drunk or used in cooking.

Although the community was much happier, nevertheless disagreements occasionally happened. One day Alice and Mary were working in a remote field. When there was no one else around Alice said, "Mary, what were you talking to my Fox about?"

Emerging from the Rubble

Mary responded, "We were discussing what would be needed for the next feast. Fox was suggesting I could sing a song."

Alice became agitated, "I think the two of you were suggesting much more than a song!"

Mary became defensive. "Honestly, that is all we talked about."

Alice grabbed Mary's dress and said, "Sing me a song now then. Demonstrate a reason why he might ask you."

Mary quivered, "You are scaring me Alice. I am not sure I can sing. I am too frightened."

Harmony said, "What's happening between you two?"

"Where did you come from?" said Alice. "I was sure no one was in sight and you could not have heard us."

"A still small voice told me you were arguing, and it brought me here," said Harmony. "What were you talking about?"

Mary said, "Alice does not believe I was only talking to Fox about singing in the festival."

Love Above All Things

Harmony said, "I know that Mary has a good voice, and I overheard the men discussing who they might like to sing next week. Alice I am sure you are mistaken if you think anything more was happening."

"I am sorry," said Alice. "I'm just a bit touchy at present. I'm not sleeping well".

"No problem," said Mary, "shall we continue?"

The two women went back to weeding the rows of carrots.

When Harmony had gone, Alice said, "How come Harmony or one of those four, always turns up just as any disagreement is happening? They seem to have a sixth sense about a voice being raised in anger."

"I know," said Mary, "but they do genuinely always seem to want to be peacemakers and they have never tried to personally benefit from the special knowledge they seem to have."

They finished their weeding and calmly walked back to the homestead.

*

Three days later the monthly thanksgiving festival was in full swing. Harmony commented to Anne

Emerging from the Rubble

that Mary had a lovely voice. Yan however, seemed concerned.

"What is it?" asked Anne.

"I have not seen the one they call Rook tonight. I have a feeling that he is avoiding the festival," said Yan. "There can't be a physical reason as Jesus is making sure that everyone keeps well. I think I'd better try to find out why he doesn't want to join us at the festival."

Yan walked to Rook's room and knocked. "Rook? Are you ok?"

After a pause Rook responded, "I did not feel like joining the party this evening. Thanks for asking."

"Happy to come in and talk if you would like," said Yan.

There was another pause and then the door opened. Rook was pleased to have company. He felt out of place at the festival because he considered that he had nothing to offer and did not have a companion to go with. Yan assured him that he was an important part of the community, and that people would like to see him at the festival. Rook thanked Yan for coming to talk, but he insisted that he would rather not go that night.

Love Above All Things

"No problem," said Yan. Then he walked back to the festival alone.

*

A few days later a young man called to his friend, "Look at this ash branch! I'm going to make a rounders bat from it."

After days of whittling, sanding, and varnishing, a finished rounders bat was used in a community rounders game one warm evening. Much to Owl's irritation, some of the scavenging expeditions brought back all sorts of balls. One week Polecat brought back a basketball and a basketball hoop. A few weeks later, a leather football was added to the growing collection. Soon there was a room dedicated to storing sports equipment and the community even formed various teams and started league tables.

Others found their voices and started a singing group, remembering as many words as they could from old songs and writing them down. One woman had a guitar presented to her by her boyfriend after a scavenging expedition, and much to her surprise, the muscle memory in her fingers could still play the chords.

Emerging from the Rubble

Time took on a new quality. People were no longer thinking about what day it was, or what month. They lived in harmony with the seasons and the weather. Without the need to constantly do things at a set time or be forever rushing to the next task, the community relaxed more and more into a holistic and connected way of living.

All was not complete harmony though. One person in the group was slowly becoming rich from storing potatoes. That person, who everyone called Magpie, had claimed a cellar, and had offered to store all the potatoes in the cellar. He knew the best way to store potatoes so that they would last for up to nine months.

Over time he persuaded the group that they should 'pay' for the potatoes that they collected from him during the winter. It was a system of barter rather than money, but it allowed Magpie to become wealthy, and he became progressively unwilling to take his turn at working in the fields, because he was able to 'pay' others to do the work for him.

"Jesus, I am concerned that some in the group are becoming rich at the expense of others who are now struggling," said Yan to Jesus on one of his return trips to Jerusalem.

Love Above All Things

Jesus replied, "Yes this has always been a problem, and will continue to be a problem for a long time even on the new earth. It will only go away when everyone has learnt to completely trust that Papa will provide all they need. Once they do, they will be willing to let go of the desire to store up wealth, by exploiting others. They will also be able to treat everyone as an equal, rather than considering how others can make them rich so that they can feel more secure."

Yan asked, "How will you achieve this?"

"On the new earth it will be achieved once sufficient Jubilee cycles have happened. There will be groups on the new earth that are similar, to begin with, to the group you are working with. They will exchange goods and services, and this will make some 'wealthy'. Every so often, Papa will declare a year of Jubilee and he will move people into new groups where they will all start again, with no possessions and no 'slaves'.

"Eventually everyone will realise that they don't have to exploit others to ensure that they have a good standard of living. They will be able to enter a state of rest. They will stop striving and be willing to enjoy the company of others, without ever considering how others might make them wealthy."

Emerging from the Rubble

Yan exclaimed, "That's amazing. I remember the concept of Jubilee that God gave to Moses, but it was never implemented as far as I know. I can see how it would work on the new earth. It will achieve a state where people can use their talents for the benefit of the community, without the desire to become rich. But, how can we stop people exploiting others in groups during this period?"

Jesus explained, "It will be achieved by causing the groups to move to a different location every so often. Sometimes a stronger group will force a weaker group to abandon their settlement, or sometimes the water supply will dry up, again forcing them to move on. It won't work perfectly, but when it has happened a number of times and people begin to trust that they will always be alright, the desire to exploit others will diminish.

"All that humans have called evil will eventually be overcome by Agape love. On the new earth, people will come to realise that they don't need to hoard possessions. Everything they need will be available to them. If they ask, they will be given.

"For example, if a musician wants a guitar, he will be given access to a person who makes guitars. When they first meet, they will agree the exact specification of the required guitar. It might take

Love Above All Things

some time for the instrument to be completed, but the person will gain the guitar they desire."

"Won't the person have to pay for the guitar?" asked Yan.

"Not through the exchange of money," replied Jesus. "Instead a relationship will be formed between the two. The first person may help the instrument maker cut and prepare the wood, or perhaps they might sing while the guitar takes shape. The craftsman will not lose or sacrifice anything. On the contrary, they will have the satisfaction of knowing another person and producing something that another person can enjoy.

"The 'currency' on the new earth is relationships not possessions. Everyone will have bodies with perfect and unlimited memories. They will have the desire to fill those memories with the knowledge of others. They will also have unlimited time to spend with others, to develop those relationships and gain insight into their lives."

"What will prevent one person exploiting another?" asked Yan.

"The desire to exploit another is a distortion of the desire to protect oneself," said Jesus. "It will take

Emerging from the Rubble

many years with some people, but eventually everyone will come to the realisation that it is better to honour others, than to exploit them.

"It will be one of your roles in the millennium and on the new earth to identify when a person is being exploited, and to shame the abuser. If necessary this should be done in front of the whole community, until they realise that it is better to respect others than exploit your fellow man."

Yan sat in deep thought for a few minutes contemplating the wonderful life the future held for everyone. "Thank you for helping me understand all this," he said to Jesus, and he then returned to the community.

6

Owl and a few of his former police officers retained a loose form of control. For many years they maintained their systems, ordering various excursions and running drills for fire, invasion and super storms. Owl still insisted on using animal names for the men. For the most part, this was respected, but over time it was seen increasingly as a quirk that belonged to Owl. Never joining in with the games, music or giving expression to his thoughts in any way, Owl started to become more and more aloof. He did, however, enjoy 'inspecting' the community. He would regularly patrol the storerooms and make notes in a little book. No one ever asked him why he did it.

Owl was incredulous at the way the community was changing. He couldn't stand the sound of laughter and singing, and so withdrew to the further reach of the apartment block and kept a silent and lonely vigil for the discipline he felt that was now lost. Despite some of the community still living in fear of his aggressive manner, most seemed to simply avoid him. This compounded

Emerging from the Rubble

his sense of futility. There were days when he felt isolated and cold inside, at such times he wondered if anyone would be sad if he was not around.

"I think this must be our thirty-fifth summer since we arrived," Yan said one evening to his friends.

The four of them had become accustomed to life in the community, but were incredibly grateful for the visits that they had been able to make to see Jesus in Jerusalem, for some respite and encouragement.

"It doesn't feel like thirty-five years though does it!" exclaimed Harmony. "Somehow time is of a quite different quality now. We don't physically age and we don't measure time the way we used to. We don't look at clocks because the batteries are long dead, and the Internet cannot govern our lives anymore!"

"We have the sun, the moon, the stars and the changing seasons," remarked Anne. "It reminds me of when I was a girl. I never knew the Internet or clocks like you two did."

"Me neither," said Thomas. "I do remember the sun dial over your door though Anne," he laughed. "Those meals we had together when you allowed

Love Above All Things

me to stay with you were such good times. We spent hours recalling all that Jesus had said only a few years before."

*

Thomas and Yan were regularly involved with the scavenging excursions. For several years, Owl did not try and bring anyone back to the camp. However, one windy autumn day, he called the men together.

"I've seen smoke rising in the distant hills. A new group must be out there. I want a team of five to go and look."

Very deliberately Owl chose Yan and Thomas, as well as Rabbit and two others.

Setting off with rations to last a few days, it was clear that Owl had appointed one of his senior guards to be in charge.

"You can call me Bull," he said.

Bull seemed happiest walking ahead of the others, as if scouting the land. Bull had an exceptionally large knife tucked into this belt. Rabbit was walking between Thomas and Yan, discussing why they had lost the last football game to the girl's team.

Emerging from the Rubble

Lagging behind was a younger man Owl had christened Stingray, due to his silent, calm, and stealthy manner.

Bull was a huge man of six foot seven. He had used his size to threaten and frighten on Owl's behalf for many years. Stingray was also an old-timer. He had arrived in the camp one day with two young women who he claimed were his sisters. It was said that they came from a farm hundreds of miles away, which had been raided by marauding scavenger gangs. His parents had been killed in front of him and his sisters.

When one of Owl's guards had taken a shine to one of his sisters, Stingray had lashed out and cut the man's throat with a kitchen knife. Far from punishing him, Owl had praised Stingray for his quick sense of justice and decisive action, and promoted him into his inner circle. Even Bull was wary of Stingray. There was something strange about him. Many thought he was dangerously unpredictable and mysterious.

"We're losing light," observed Bull, setting down his pack. "Let's get ready to camp here tonight."

"I'll get some firewood," said Thomas.

"I'll prepare the food with Stingray," said Yan.

Love Above All Things

Stingray calmly walked over to Yan and stood only inches from him, face to face. He shook his head slowly and menacingly.

Yan looked into Stingray's eyes and he could feel the anger, but behind the anger there seemed to be fear.

Stingray dropped his pack and pulled out a heavy tarpaulin. He shook it open and spread it on the ground. It was clear that he knew what he wanted to do. The look on his face demonstrated that he was angry at being told what to do by Yan.

"We should be in the hills by mid-morning tomorrow," said Bull. There were now three plumes of smoke rising from the crest of a hill on the horizon.

After a mainly silent meal of canned fish and flatbreads warmed by a fire, the men settled down to sleep. Thomas, Yan and Rabbit had drifted off into a deep slumber next to the fire, whilst Stingray and Bull took first watch.

The night dragged on. The moon was up, but was only making brief appearances between thick wedges of cloud that were scurrying across the night sky in the wind. Bull and Stingray had fallen asleep, without waking the others for their shift. A

Emerging from the Rubble

twig snapping startled Bull, and before his eyes could become accustomed to the dark, teeth had sunk into his neck.

Suddenly awakened by the sound of Bull screaming and gagging, Stingray leapt up. Grabbing Bull's knife from his belt, Stingray pushed it hard into the black creature that was subsuming Bull. The animal let out a terrific roar of pain and stood up to full height, letting Bull go. Bull fell back, clutching his neck. The black bear turned its attention to Stingray. Towering over his slight frame, the bear brought its full weight down on Stingray, knocking him to the ground like a ragdoll.

Its huge paws pinned Stingray to the ground and with a horrifying crunch of teeth on bone, the bear took a chunk of flesh out of Stingray's left shoulder and lower neck. Stingray screamed as his arms flailed, trying to push the bear away.

Everyone was now awake. Yan scrambled over to where man and beast were engaged in a struggle for life. Yan lay over Stingray's torso as the bear tried to push him out of the way.

Bull grabbed a long and sturdy stick and thrashed at the fire, sending red hot embers into the bear's fur. The bear reared up in pain as the embers

Love Above All Things

seared its flesh. Although in pain himself Bull frantically pounded the fire with the stick, until the bear backed away from Yan and Stingray. With a shout, Bull ran at the bear which had turned on its heel and had begun to run back into the surrounding trees, moaning in pain as it fled.

Painfully Yan got on to his knees as Thomas shone a light onto Stingray. Thick crimson blood was oozing steadily from what was left of Stingray's left shoulder. Yan did his best to put pressure on the wound, but the wound was bigger than both of his hands.

Thomas threw him a spare T-shirt. "Try this!" he panted as he searched the edge of the darkened trees for signs of a reprisal attack.

Rabbit moved anxiously over to Bull.

"Let me see?"

Bull removed his hand from his neck. Puncture wounds were bleeding on the back of his neck.

"Thankfully, your artery and spine were missed," said Rabbit. "You'll be ok." Rabbit placed his hand on Bull's shoulder, in a simple act of solidarity.

Bull came to Stingray's side. "You saved my life."

Emerging from the Rubble

Stingray's eyes, full of fear, met Bull's. Breathing heavily, Stingray was squirming. Bull removed his coat and put it under Stingray's head.

"I... I... took a life..." he spluttered, blood beginning to soak Bull's jacket.

"You saved my life," repeated Bull, his eyes filled with gratitude and concern.

Yan grasped Stingray's hand. "You were very brave," said Yan gently.

Stingray looked at Yan and coughed up a mouthful of blood.

"I'm so cold," whispered Stingray.

"Do you want to be healed?" asked Thomas.

Stingray nodded.

Thomas looked at Yan. Yan knew what Thomas was asking.

"It's the right thing," Yan said without hesitation.

Thomas bowed his head slightly and closed his eyes, with both of his hands placed on the mangled flesh.

In a strange act of intuition, Stingray placed his hand on top of Thomas's. With a faint gurgle in his voice he croaked, "Carlos. My name is Carlos."

Love Above All Things

Thomas nodded without opening his eyes. A few silent moments ebbed before Carlos began to breath heavily, his chest heaving up and down. He coughed and a small amount of dark blood came out of his mouth. He cleared his throat, "What are you doing?" he asked, the ghost of a smile on his face, like a quizzical child.

Thomas's eyes remained shut, and a gentle smile was beginning to form on his face too. Under his bloodied hands, flesh was moving. Muscle sinews and blood vessels snaked in a mysterious dance, reconnecting and fusing together. Within a minute, skin was being knit back together. Carlos began to wriggle as if he was being tickled. Suddenly he let out an explosive laugh.

"What the hell?" gasped Bull. Rabbit stood next to him, rubbing his chin under his open mouth.

"Help him sit up Yan," Thomas said, shaking the blood from his hands. Yan pulled Carlos upright.

"Eeeeee," Rabbit squeaked, expecting a howl of pain from Carlos. Carlos looked down at his shoulder.

Yan crouched next to Carlos. He poured water over the shoulder, wiping away the residual blood

Emerging from the Rubble

on the bare skin. A perfectly healed shoulder was soon revealed.

"How?" said Carlos, with a mixture of shock and immense relief.

Yan, still crouching by his side offered an explanation. "We are friends with Jesus. He has gifted us his healing power. But, please, we must ask you to say nothing about this. We are not here to use gifts like this to make anyone do anything, only to demonstrate the love that Jesus has for everyone."

Bull had a quizzical look on his face reflecting his conflicting emotions. Fear, excitement and relief were pumping around his body with the adrenaline arising from the bear attack.

"Jesus?" asked Bull, his voice quivering slightly. "How? I've never really understood what Jesus is all about?"

Thomas smiled warmly. "No one can really understand everything about him, but, put simply, he has shown us how to live to our full potential. I know him quite well, and all he has ever done is to show us how to allow his love to flow through us."

Love Above All Things

"How can you know him?" asked Bull, genuinely. "Hasn't he been dead for thousands of years?"

"That's a story for another time," said Thomas. "Come on, let's keep moving. The animals are still obviously aggressive toward humankind around here."

"Can you blame them after all we've done to this planet?" said Rabbit.

After a further hike of several more miles, the men found an old petrol station and hunkered down on the floor in the old shop building to try to get some more sleep.

Carlos deliberately made his bed near to Thomas and Yan.

"Please. Tell me everything, friends. Tell me." With tears in his eyes, he reached out his hand and Thomas took it.

"I will, in time," reassured Thomas. "You're going to be alright, you know," he said kindly.

For the first time ever in his life, Carlos believed it.

A peaceful sleep fell upon the five of them and they slept until long after dawn.

Emerging from the Rubble

The sunlight shone brightly on Carlos's face. His first thought as he awoke was how beautiful the sunlight made everything look. Then he remembered what had happened in the night, and flexed his shoulder. Joy bubbled up inside his torso, and for the first time in his life he felt as if he was being held by some invisible hands. He felt a surge of conviction deep within him that existence was meaningful, and that he was worthy of being loved.

He raised his head and noticed Thomas and Yan who were standing just outside the door of the building. They weren't talking to each other, but were simply standing still, their faces lifted toward the sun. Carlos knew that he wanted to join them.

Thomas turned to Carlos with a broad smile and put an arm around his healed shoulders. No words were needed. Carlos began to weep. At first it was just a silent stream of tears, but within a minute he was sobbing. Years of emotion came flooding to the surface. It was as if a dam had burst. Yan and Thomas held him as he wept. This was a moment of great inner release.

Before long, Rabbit and Bull had made their way outside. Without wanting to create an awkward situation, they had waited quietly until Carlos was

Love Above All Things

ready, and the group could begin the final push toward the mountain top. Smoke had once again begun to rise, which was an indication that breakfast was being prepared up there.

7

Owl sat at his desk. He drummed his fingers while deep in thought.

"Are you sure you won't join us?" Anne persisted.

She sat with Sylvia and Harmony opposite Owl. They had sought an audience with him. There were no men patrolling the apartment block, nor guards on the door.

Owl remained silent, glaring at Anne with a stern expression on his face.

Anne looked into Owl's eyes, searching for a glimmer of warmth. Owl was rarely seen in the courtyard now and had taken up residence in his lobby office almost permanently. He still tried to feign an air of superiority and control, but in reality, his world had fallen apart.

"Your colleagues let us know that it's your one hundredth birthday, and we have found enough ingredients to make you a cake! Please come and have some with us?" Sylvia did her best to break through the icy exterior of the community's patriarch.

Love Above All Things

Finally, Owl spoke, "I am in no need of celebration." His expression was so wooden it was almost surreal.

Harmony surmised that Owl was experiencing conflicting emotions. She knew that Owl craved recognition and to be included in the community, but these were not his preferred terms. She attempted a different approach.

"Sir, you have protected this community for so long. You have given your life to serve this city. We want to honour you on your birthday. You deserve a party!"

Harmony did not realise how incensed Owl would become when she used the word party.

"That's all this place has become!" Owl erupted, swiping his arm across the desk, causing a mug, an old lamp and an ashtray to smash on to the floor.

"A party! Where is the discipline? Where is the order? Where is the respect?"

The three women suddenly felt unsafe and quickly stood up to leave.

"Where are you going?" screamed Owl, his rage now coming to the fore. "I haven't finished! Since

Emerging from the Rubble

you two arrived I have watched this community become soft. Do you know what it takes to survive in this world?"

Anne felt a tidal wave of anger swell within her. She shot a short prayer heavenwards for self-control.

"Owl, we are thriving. Don't you see? The seeds we planted years ago have allowed us to build a working farmstead. We are eating well. We are growing more than enough. The people are happy. They are happy with each other and laughing. Owl, this has all happened on your watch."

Anne bravely waited for Owl's response. Harmony and Sylvia stood by her side.

Sylvia continued, summoning all her courage. "Before we were afraid," she said. "Now we are not. You have given this place back to us, and we are so happy."

Owl felt the temptation to crumble. He could imagine two paths forward. One was offering him a chance to let go and join in the celebration. The other choice was to remain firm and hold on to his sense of dignity. All the years of struggle, suffering, fear and the personal cost to him flashed through his mind. Before he could process everything

Love Above All Things

rationally, he started to speak. "That's right!" he spat. "I have given every ounce of my being to protect this group. If we go soft, we fucking die!" Owl felt hot justification pump through him, which pushed him even further into his own rhetoric.

"Who regrouped what was left of the police? Who fought off marauding gangs of looters? Who marshalled the people into efficient teams, so that we could survive this long?"

The more he screamed, the more he allowed every justification to become his reasoning. It was like he was disappearing into his own construct of who he thought he was.

"Ok Owl. We cannot force you to come, but please know you are welcome, and we will be honouring you." Anne was determined to remain calm in the face of Owl's fury.

The three women calmly walked out of the lobby office.

Owl was left short of breath. He slumped onto a chair, unlocked a drawer under the desk and reached for a cigarette. These were in very short supply, so he only had one when he felt particularly overwhelmed.

Emerging from the Rubble

Alone and smoking slowly, Owl shut the doors to anyone and anything. After a few minutes, he climbed the stairs and walked up on to the roof of the apartment block. He always went there when he wanted to survey the community.

"I built this," he muttered under his breath, exhaling the stale smoke from his tired lungs. A movement caught his eye. In the fields behind the complex, he could see Polecat tending to the crops. Polecat was singing to himself whilst fixing some newly repaired piping to the irrigation system he had built.

Owl felt a crushing sense of hatred toward Polecat. "Look at that lanky piece of shit!" he growled to no-one but himself. "He'd be dead without me, the ungrateful dog."

Looking down on the other side of the apartments and on to the courtyard he saw people milling about. Some were playing a game of chequers with white and grey pebbles, and a couple sat romantically together, their limbs overlapping. In the corner, he saw Anne, Harmony and Sylvia congratulating a young man and woman on the largest cake he had ever seen.

The sight of that cake caused Owl to have a sudden realisation that he was consumed with a desperate darkness, unable to let himself enjoy the simple birthday gift. He realised his own bleak capability for hatred, and then experienced a sense of clarity. In a stunning moment of relief, he realised that he didn't need to feel like that anymore.

Owl took a final deep pull on his cigarette, calmly stepped on the butt, walked to the edge of the roof, and fell forward. In the two seconds of falling, Owl finally felt free of all burdens. Then his head met the concrete beneath, and with a violently loud crack his body shattered, then lay still.

*

Polecat heard a loud thud and looked over to the source of the sound. A cloud of dust had been caused by something that had seemed to fall from the roof. Intrigued, he wandered over to investigate. As the dust settled, Polecat realised that the crumpled heap on the ground was Owl. Blood was trickling from his ears and a gaping wound was open across his head. Blood and brain matter were now matting his hair.

Polecat had seen lots of bloodied bodies, but there was something strange about this one. Owl's face was turned to the side, but his expression

Emerging from the Rubble

was strangely peaceful. Polecat felt a confusing mixture of sadness and relief. This was a man who had beaten him, and bullied him. A man who had been feared far more than respected. However, this was a man who had used all of his energy to preserve a community as it had emerged from the rubble.

Unsure what he should do, Polecat stood for a while, watching the blood mingle with the dusty earth. He decided it was best to go and tell everyone.

Climbing up on a chair, Polecat cupped his hands over his mouth.

"Listen everyone," he called out. "I have something important to tell you."

After a few seconds, the courtyard turned quiet, waiting for his announcement.

"Owl is dead," proclaimed Polecat.

There was a loud, audible gasp from many in the community.

"It seems that he jumped from the roof."

Anne and Harmony looked at each other, unsure of what to think.

Love Above All Things

Sylvia spoke up first. "So there we are. He couldn't live without being in control." Her words were devoid of emotion as she stared into the distance.

There was an exodus from the courtyard as everyone followed Polecat out to see the body.

"We did all we could do," Harmony reassured Anne.

Anne nodded, but looked sad. "We could not reach him," she murmured. "What will Jesus say? Did we fail?"

"Did I reach everyone, when I first came?" Anne turned around to see Jesus standing behind her.

Jesus gave Anne a reassuring hug.

"Of course not!" answered Anne, wiping tears of relief from her eyes. "Many did not understand your message."

"And so," replied Jesus, "Javert couldn't let his training and conditioning go."

"Javert? Was that his real name?" asked Harmony.

"Yes. He was nicknamed Owl affectionately by his former superior, because he seemed to see clearly when everything seemed confusing and dark."

Emerging from the Rubble

"Where is Owl now?" asked Anne.

"He'll be resurrected when Papa says so. His story is by no means over. We never give up on anyone." Jesus gave one of his reassuring smiles. He sat and motioned for Anne and Harmony to sit with him.

"Death only happens now when an individual resolves to take their own life, or a life is taken by force. Let me ask you, how do you see this community going forward?"

Harmony offered her thoughts. "Things are so much better. Lightness and laughter are returning."

"Where will the people look now for direction?" asked Jesus.

Harmony and Anne thought for a minute.

"I don't know for sure," said Harmony. "They will want a new leader, but the process of deciding who that will be could be complicated."

"It will take a long time for the ingrained desires and characteristics to soften. Be patient with them. Do your best to be peacemakers. I know you love them all," Jesus advised.

Jesus reassured the friends further, then he told them he had to leave.

Love Above All Things

"Who was that?" asked Sylvia.

"That was Jesus," replied Anne.

"Where did he come from?"

"Jesus goes wherever he is needed. He's an old friend of ours."

"I feel like I know him," said Sylvia, looking puzzled.

"You kind of do," laughed Harmony. "We all do."

Sylvia seemed satisfied with such an abstract answer and she was happy to have seen Jesus.

8

The sun was now at the zenith of its arc for the day, and the men were sweating as they climbed an exposed road, which zig-zagged up the mountain side. Every few hundred yards there were reminders of the great migration – discarded gas bottles, broken down vehicles which were slowly rusting, and sometimes there were even the lonely remains of an unfortunate traveller, their bones bleached by exposure to the elements.

Despite the fatigue from constant walking, the mood of the five of them was good. Carlos was getting used to being called by his real name again.

Rabbit and Bull were deep in discussion...

"So, what do you think? Magic? Are they witchdoctors? How can they make flesh heal so perfectly?" Rabbit was mystified by who these men were, especially after he had also been impacted by the kindness of their female friends. It was beginning to bother him constantly, that these people were so different, and yet so unassuming.

Love Above All Things

"Possible I guess," said Bull in response. "I've never met a witchdoctor before. What do they do?"

"They commune with the spirit world, and tap into its power," said Rabbit, animated by the idea.

"I don't think I believe in a spirit world," said Bull, "I was always told to only trust things that could be proven."

"So what was last night, if not proof? I'm going to ask them. I have to know who the hell we are dealing with!" said Rabbit, his intrigue beginning to overwhelm him.

Bull wanted to protest, but couldn't think of a good enough reason. He opened his mouth but no words came. Before Bull realised Rabbit had caught up to Yan and Thomas ahead of him.

"So, I have to know. Who and what are you?"

Thomas knew what he meant and didn't try and evade the question.

"We are travellers. We are old friends. We are followers of 'The Way'."

"What 'Way'?" replied Rabbit, excited at the thought of finding out more about why Thomas

Emerging from the Rubble

and his friends behaved in unusual ways sometimes.

"The Way of Truth and Life," Yan pitched in.

"What Truth? Whose Life?" challenged Rabbit. A smile was growing across his face at the progress he felt he was making.

"The universal truth of what life is about. Your life, my life, everyone's existence. There is a true meaning to why we are here." Thomas felt able to share this information because Rabbit was being so genuine. Carlos listened intently as he walked alongside. Bull joined them and they discussed the meaning of truth and life.

"I used to think that life had meaning, but when my family were taken from me, it felt like the universe was a cold and cruel place. Can you understand that?" Rabbit said, with a sense of relief to finally voice his pain.

"Yes, I believe the soul of the universe understands that completely," responded Yan. "In fact, I believe no one has experienced rejection like the soul of the universe. Imagine you have a thousand children and only a handful ever cared about you? The rest of them abused what you gave them,

Love Above All Things

ignored your loving advice, and cursed your name? How would you feel?"

Rabbit was stunned by the question. He had never entertained the idea that the consciousness itself could have feelings, and experience pain.

"When you say, 'soul of the universe', do you mean God?" Bull asked.

"That word is so clumsy," laughed Thomas. "The word 'God' means so many things to so many people. Many millions of lives have been ruined in the cause of 'God', by religious ideologies over the centuries. But beyond religion and dogma, the universe is alive with consciousness and love. Yan and I have been called by this love. It is absolutely unfailing love. It cannot and does not give up on anyone."

Bull pondered and then continued, "So, does this consciousness control things?"

"No, and yes," said Yan. "No, it doesn't violate our choices. It doesn't micromanage creation. However, it is working through us to make all things better. It is like a good father, always working towards his children being safe and happy, but not invading their every moment or making them a puppet."

Emerging from the Rubble

Carlos was intrigued, "So how did you heal my shoulder?"

"Healing is a power that has been gifted to some, so that they can demonstrate God's love. If we use this gift for our glory or to give us power, we would be abusing it. Love doesn't seek glory for itself. It only seeks to benefit others." Thomas said, remembering the things he had learnt about healing from Jesus all those years ago.

Carlos wanted to share his thoughts. "I felt held last night as I went to sleep. I felt like the universe was for me, and not against me. I felt that I was cherished and reassured, that I am going to be alright!"

Thomas chuckled with delight, "Yes, that is the feeling of being loved. The soul of the universe is a good and loving father who holds us all. He will not disrespect our autonomy, but he will always be with us, to encourage us to give and receive love."

"If I can tell you one thing," added Yan, "it is that the future is full of bright hope. All things will be well."

The men were reaching the summit of the hill. Taking a minute to look back at the distance they had travelled, they could see the great city stretched out like a huge grey blanket on the land. On the edge of the city they could make out the district where the apartment block was situated, and they each silently thought of their friends who were there.

Turning back toward the summit, they could now smell the smoke which they had been able to see their entire journey.

"We are close," said Bull.

He led the five men forward into a dense pine forest through which a road had been cut. Preferring the cover of trees, Bull was utilising his experience in the army, to stay hidden from view, while they discovered the origin of the smoke.

In the distance they could glimpse a camp in a clearing, a short distance from the road. Two huge trucks were parked on the roadside.

"Electric vehicles!" exclaimed Carlos. "I haven't seen a working vehicle for decades! Wow, and they have large solar panels to recharge them."

The clearing was surrounded by several tarpaulin constructions. A large fire was burning in the middle of the clearing. Two men were piling wood onto it.

Emerging from the Rubble

"Guns," said Bull quietly, pointing at a group of men who were standing smoking at the edge of the clearing, carrying automatic rifles. "And cigarettes!" added Rabbit.

"All of these things are so rare now. That can only mean that they are ruthless at taking whatever they find," said Bull in a serious tone.

"They are likely to head our way," said Carlos with trepidation.

"What now, holy boys?" said Bull with a sarcastic, but not unfriendly air.

"I think we have to proceed very cautiously," said Yan.

Bull nodded and looked at Thomas. "Anything to add, witchdoctor?"

Thomas thought for a second. On the one hand he wanted to reach out to them now but, on the other hand, he wanted to avoid anything dangerous happening.

"What would Owl say?" asked Rabbit, not knowing that Owl was now dead.

"Owl would want us to batten down the hatches and protect ourselves," remarked Bull. "Remember when we fought off the last gang of raiders?"

Love Above All Things

Carlos and Rabbit were wistful and looked sad as they recalled the battle which had raged, resulting in many of their community being killed.

"I do think we need to take a closer look at what they have at any rate," said Bull. "Rabbit, let's get closer and have a look."

Rabbit didn't protest. He was keen to get moving.

Creeping around the edge of the clearing, Bull and Rabbit could see about twenty men carrying various weapons, pistols, meat cleavers, shotguns and automatic rifles. They were mostly heavily bearded, wearing sunglasses and looked strong and healthy.

Rabbit was surveying a group sitting on the ground, who were eating from some tins, when his heart almost stopped.

Bull heard his sudden intake of breath. "What's up?" he asked.

"I think. I think that's my son!" gasped Rabbit loudly.

"Shhhhhh!" hissed Bull.

"It's my boy, Ally!" said Rabbit, beginning to cry.

Bull heaved a sigh, acknowledging that things were going to get complicated.

Emerging from the Rubble

Rabbit's strong emotions as a father made him instinctively want to run and embrace his son, Ally. Bull sensed this, and laid a heavy hand on his shoulder. "Rabbit, mate. Don't do it! Look at all those weapons!"

In the middle-distance Ally turned, and Rabbit and Bull could clearly see that Ally was missing an arm.

"What happened to him?" gasped Rabbit as he sobbed.

"Let's go. Come on!" urged Bull, practically dragging Rabbit away.

After several minutes of frantic scrambling, the two men found Yan and Thomas sitting with Carlos.

"My boy! My boy was there! He... his arm..."

Thomas nodded in understanding. "Look at me," he said calmly. "What else did you see?"

Bull stepped in, "Weapons. A lot of them. We have to go!"

Yan looked at Thomas, and in that quiet moment they were united in thought.

"Let's get back and report on what we've seen," suggested Thomas. "We will have to make some decisions as a community."

Love Above All Things

"Don't you think Owl will immediately impose stricter controls?" asked Carlos as they began to walk quickly back out of the woodland and on to the road.

"Without a doubt," sighed Bull.

"What choice do we have!" exclaimed Rabbit. "As soon as they see signs of life at our camp, they will invade. Any resistance and it will be a bloodbath!"

Thomas and Yan remained silent, listening to the worries of their friends as they walked determinedly back to the camp.

Adrenaline sped them on their journey. During and after the seven years of great turmoil, violent gangs had formed to try and seize the resources that remained. For years they had fought first the diminished state forces, and then each other. Now only the toughest survived.

"Do you think the threat is real?" Yan quietly asked Thomas.

"I am sure it is. I think we both know what we need to do."

"Convince Owl and his men to leave the camp?" asked Yan.

Emerging from the Rubble

"Yes, exactly. It's the only way we know we can definitely avoid bloodshed. If we go back into the forest on the other side of the valley, I think we can maintain a vantage point to watch their activity, and see if they find the camp."

Yan thought for a moment, realising how much of an upheaval it would be to have to start again somewhere else.

"I have no doubt that they will find the camp," he said with resignation. "The fields are so well farmed now around the apartments, that they will be able to see us the moment they come out of the woods."

"We have to pray that Owl will listen to our suggestion and that he goes along with us. He could really make things difficult if he wants everyone to stay and defend the camp!"

Eventually, the tired men arrived back at the camp. Anne was delighted and relieved to see them, and she and Harmony rushed to greet them.

Thomas could see from their faces that something was awry. A wordless hug was followed by Anne breaking the news.

"Owl is dead," she said with sadness in her eyes.

Love Above All Things

The group of men looked at each other, uneasy at how to respond.

"How?" asked Bull, squinting in the sunlight.

"Jumped from the roof," said Harmony. "Died instantly."

The seven of them rounded the corner and walked into the field where the entire community was gathered. A mound of earth covered the remains of the once revered leader of the camp. Some of the older men looked genuinely grieved, and whilst everyone kept a respectful hush, it was also clear that there was a sense of relief in the air.

The men joined the group in quiet remembrance.

"What of the smoke?" asked one lady, turning to Thomas.

Thomas looked at her, full of compassion and then stepped up on to a bench. Every face turned toward him, and he had the complete attention of the entire community.

"Friends. This is a difficult moment for us all. We have returned to find Owl has left us, and we have returned with news of what we saw in the mountains. I believe we have to make a very

Emerging from the Rubble

tough choice, urgently." Thomas paused and surveyed the scores of faces, looking to him for guidance.

"There is a group on the mountain. They seem to be a gang of marauders."

Suddenly, uninvited, Bull climbed up next to Thomas. "They are very heavily armed," he declared.

A gasp went up from the crowd.

Thomas considered the fact that he was now not alone on the makeshift stage. He decided to honour Bull and present a united front.

"Bull and Rabbit went close to their camp and saw their weapons stash at close quarters."

The people looked at Bull and some nodded their heads in respect.

Bull folded his arms, satisfied with the feeling of influence he was now enjoying.

"The moment they leave their makeshift camp and emerge from the woods, they will see our work in the fields. We can expect them to be here within twenty-four hours," Bull continued.

A murmur of distress spread across the courtyard.

Love Above All Things

"I believe we should fight for our homestead," suggested Bull, loudly. "This is our city. Our settlement. We have put our lives into this place. I say we use what we can to defend it. Who is with me?"

Thomas was quick to quell the murmur by continuing. "I believe the best chance for us all is to leave this place and head for the opposite side of the valley. Our hope is that they will move in here for a while, and then move on. From a new camp, we can watch them and return here should they travel on. But friends, I must tell you, I think we should prepare to leave with the knowledge that it may never be safe to return.

"As you know, I have no wish to be recognised or rewarded as your leader, but, if you choose this path, I will help you all during these coming years and promise to always act in the interests of the whole community to the best of my ability."

The crowd remained awkwardly quiet. Bull grimaced at Thomas.

"Bull has made his proposal. I have made mine," said Thomas. "Neither option is easy by any means. Bull, I understand your desire to protect this place that we have all come to call home.

Emerging from the Rubble

"As a community we now must decide, do we fight for what we have accomplished, or do we leave in silence in the face of those wishing to crucify us?"

Rabbit moved forward and addressed the community. "We've got to decide quickly. Are you with Bull or with Thomas?"

There was a moment's silence, then Carlos shouted, "Thomas". Then Polecat shouted, "Thomas". More and more voices were heard, and they all shouted, "Thomas!"

Postscript

If you would like to comment on the issues raised in the story do join one of our discussion groups, look us up on:

Facebook we have a group called *Love Above All Things*.

MeWe where we also have a group called *Love Above All Things*.

Twitter @laattweet or

Instagram @laatinsta

We will be posting articles and more information about future projects on the web site http://www.loveaboveallthings.org

Further Reading

If you wish to explore the topics raised in this book in more detail you may find the following books useful:

God Can't: How to Believe in God and Love after Tragedy, Abuse, and Other Evils

by Thomas Jay Oord

People often ask heart-felt questions about God and suffering. Frequently the usual answers fail. They don't support the truth that God loves everyone all the time. God Can't seeks to give an answer to why a good and powerful God doesn't prevent evil.

Grace Saves All

by David Artman

David Artman argues that grace saves alone and goes to all. He contends that the inclusive / Christian universalist approach is necessary because it offers the only Christian theology which successfully defends the goodness of God. For it logically follows that if God is all-good, all-knowing, and all-powerful, then God must also be all-saving.

Love Above All Things

Her Gates Will Never Be Shut: Hell, Hope, and the New Jerusalem

by Bradley Jersak

Would the God of love revealed by Jesus really consign the vast majority of humankind to a destiny of eternal, conscious torment? Is divine mercy bound by the demands of justice? How can anyone presume to know who is saved from the flames and who is not? If there is a God who loves us, then surely all are welcome into the heavenly kingdom, regardless of their beliefs or behaviors in this life.

How Wide Are Heaven's Doors?: The Biblical Case for Ultimate Restoration

by George W. Sarris

This short book is designed to briefly introduce people to information from Church history and the teaching of the Bible that has been misunderstood, misinterpreted and misrepresented to show that what most people have been told about the nature and duration of hell is not true. George Sarris asserts that the true teaching of the Bible is that God will one day restore all of His creation to the perfection He initially intended.

Emerging from the Rubble

If Grace Is True: Why God Will Save Every Person

by Philip Gulley and James Mulholland

For seekers, for thoughtful Christians, and for the simply curious, Gulley and Mulholland offer a beautiful, timeless message of hope. Long disturbed by the Church's struggle between offering both love and rejection, they discover what God wants from us and for us: grace for everyone.

Raising Hell: Christianity's Most Controversial Doctrine Put Under Fire

by Julie Ferwerda

If you've ever had doubts or questions about the incompatibility of eternal torment with a merciful God, Raising Hell will open your eyes to a radical view of God's loving purpose for all humanity and what the "Good News" is really about.

Love Above All Things

That All Shall Be Saved: Heaven, Hell, and Universal Salvation

by David Bentley Hart

In this momentous book, David Bentley Hart makes the case that nearly two millennia of dogmatic tradition have misled readers on the crucial matter of universal salvation. On the basis of the earliest Christian writings, theological tradition, scripture, and logic, Hart argues that if God is the good creator of all, he is the savior of all, without fail. With great rhetorical power, wit, and emotional range, Hart offers a new perspective on one of Christianity's most important themes.

The Inescapable Love of God

by Thomas Talbott

Will the love of God save us all? In this book Thomas Talbott seeks to expose the extent to which the Western theological tradition has managed to twist the New Testament message of love, forgiveness, and hope into a message of fear and guilt.

Author Profiles

David Bell and Dave Griffiths offer their first book 'Emerging from the Rubble'. It has been created from their joint passion to spread the message of hope for all as promised by our loving Father.

David Bell has been retired for over ten years. He has devoted much of his retirement to a detailed study of the prophesies in the bible. He was raised in a Christian family and has attended churches of many denominations. David has three children, two stepchildren and three grandchildren.

Dave Griffiths is a musician by night and family minister by day. He has released several critically acclaimed albums with his bands Bosh and Chaos Curb, as well as solo work. He graduated from Moorlands College with a BA in Applied Theology and is currently a Family Minister in his local parish. Dave has a passion for theology, all things creative and lives with his wife Jess, three kids, two cats and one dog in Dorset, England.